MW00909942

This
Welcome to School Book
is especially for

_____

from
Family Reading Partnership
made possible with support from
M&T Bank

Family Reading Partnership

Wishing you many hours of family reading
fun and a wonderful kindergarten year!
www.familyreading.org

Text and illustrations copyright © 2013
by Katrina Morse
Layout and design by Katrina Morse
www.katrinamorse.com

All rights reserved.
ISBN-13: 978-0-9896964-0-1

Illustrations are rendered in acrylic paint and colored pencil.

It Began with a Song

written and illustrated by
Katrina Morse

One day a bird sang a song.

la

La   la.

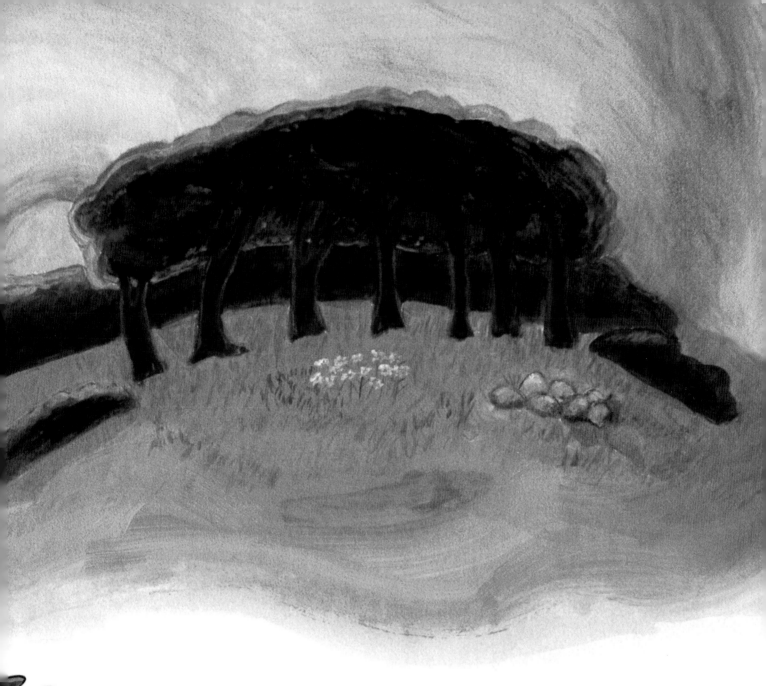

And then...

All the trees swayed,

first left, then right, what a sight!

The daisy patch woke
and each flower
s t r e t c h e d ,

A little bee buzzed to the tune in the air.

Buzzz, buzzz!

One mole heard the morning
and started to hum.

Hummm,
hum, humm.

Two snakes felt the beat

and nodded their heads

up

and down.

up

and down.

Three rabbits hopped high
in the bright yellow sun.

BOING!

BOING!

BOING!

Four gray furry squirrels circled
'round and around!

Zim, zam, ZOOOm!

The fox family pranced
and wagged their five tails.
Wiggy wag.

A big ole brown bear
put her paws in the air.

CLAP. CLAP.

Buzzz!

The wind swept around
and kissed all its friends
on their cheeks.

Kiss,

The sun shone its rays in a warm embrace,

such a *hug*,

Ahhhhhhh...

Everyone felt the music and moved,
Up and down here, around about there.

Hurray! Let's dance!

And to think all along
it began with a song.
La, la, la!

Meadow Song and Dance

by Katrina Morse © 2013

More Fun!

Make Up Your Own Dance
Can you move like a snake? Can you hop like a rabbit? How would a bear dance? Move like the wind does. Do a sunshine dance.

Be an Explorer
Go outside and start looking. How many shapes of leaves can you find? Are there long skinny grass leaves? Can you find any heart-shaped or oval-shaped leaves? Do you see any animals or insects? How does it look different outside in the different seasons?

Tell a Story
• What adventures would you have if you were a mole? Imagine what you do in your home underground. Tell a story about it.
• Pretend you are a rock outside. Imagine what happens around you during the day and then during the night.
• Do you think it would be fun to be able to fly like a bird? Imagine where you would go if you had wings and could soar in the sky.

Create Your Own Book
Make your own book by folding pieces of paper in half and putting them together. Draw a picture on each page to tell the story. How does your story begin? What happens in the middle? How does it end?

About the Author-Artist

Katrina Morse loves to paint, create, explore, dance, and pet her cats. She lives in the beautiful Finger Lakes region of upstate New York where the diversity of the people and the natural world inspire her imagination.

You can find out more about her graphic design work, paintings, and other children's books at www.katrinamorse.com.